P9-ARQ-958

DATE DUE

PRINTED IN U.S.A.

Welcome to 4B

Brynn Kelly

FX: 1-24

An imprint of Enslow Publishing

WEST **44** BOOKS™

THE BAD KiDS IN 4B

Welcome to 4B

Things That Don't Make Sense

Detention Is a Lot Like Jail

Cutting Through the Noise

Please visit our website, www.west44books.com.
For a free color catalog of all our high-quality books,
call toll free 1-800-542-2595 or fax 1-877-542-2596.

Cataloging-in-Publication Data

Names: Kelly, Brynn.
Title: Welcome to 4B / Brynn Kelly.
Description: New York : West 44, 2019. | Series: The bad kids in 4B
Identifiers: ISBN 9781538382219 (pbk.) | ISBN 9781538382226
 (library bound) | ISBN 9781538383117 (ebook)
Subjects: LCSH: Schools--Juvenile fiction. | Families--Juvenile fiction. |
 Friendship--Juvenile fiction.
Classification: LCC PZ7.K455 We 2019 | DDC [E]--dc23

First Edition

Published in 2019 by
Enslow Publishing LLC
101 West 23rd Street, Suite #240
New York, NY 10011

Copyright © 2019 Enslow Publishing LLC

Editor: Theresa Emminizer
Designer: Seth Hughes

Printed in the United States of America

CPSIA compliance information: Batch #CS18W44: For further information contact
Enslow Publishing LLC, New York, New York at 1-800-542-2595.

THE BAD KIDS IN 4B

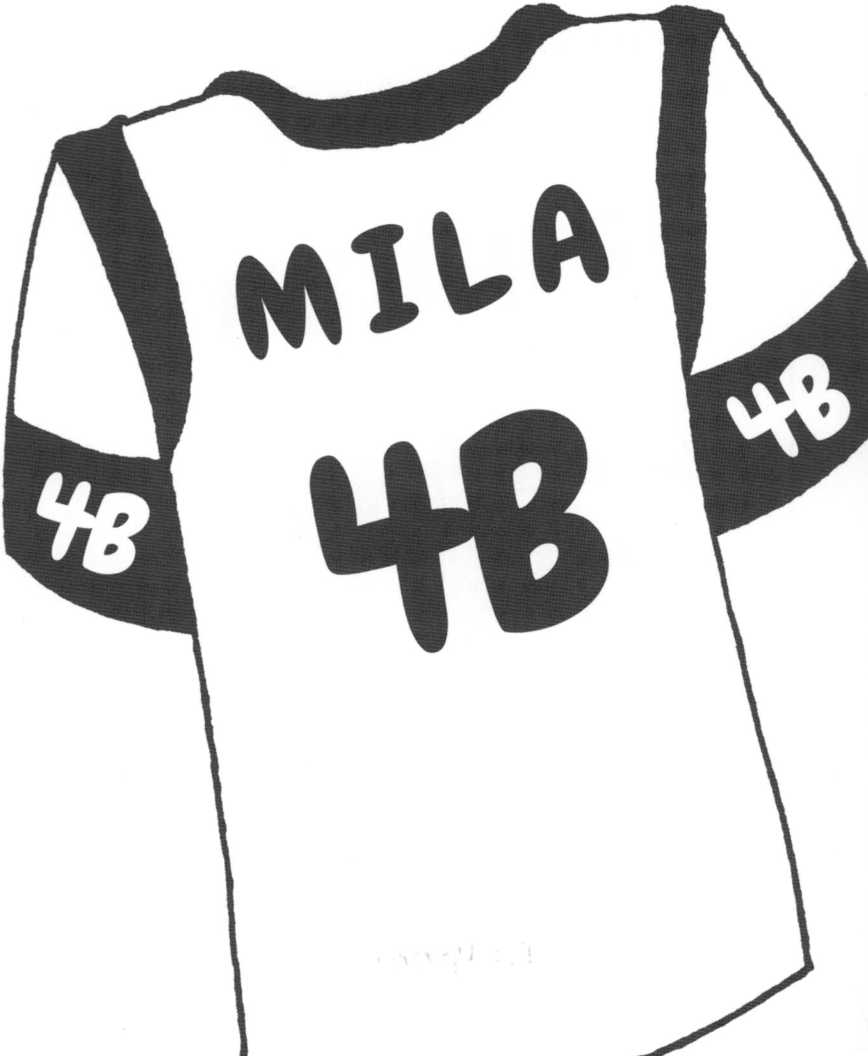
MILA
48
48
48

DETENTION SLIP

NAME Mila Hernandez

DATE October 4th

GRADE 7th

TEACHER Mrs. Marks

REASON Mila would not follow directions when I asked her to pay attention in class. She yelled that my husband died to get away from me.

Chapter One:
A Bad Week

Mila followed the principal down the hall. He was taking her to room 4B. She had heard that classroom was for bad kids. She was not a bad kid! Okay, she did make Mrs. Marks cry. But, she was having a very bad week. The worst week of her life. No one could blame her for being upset.

Mila looked into the other classrooms as she walked. The kids were working together and talking. *They all look happy*, she thought. She was sure their lives were easier. None of them had left their friends and old school behind.

"Here we are, Mila." Mr. Stride stopped in front of a closed door. He reached for the doorknob. "Miss Andrews is the teacher for 4B. She'll be your new seventh-grade teacher while you're here."

Mila hated Mr. Stride. She hated how quickly he judged her. He thought she was a troublemaker. That was not true. She was a good student. But Mrs. Marks would *not* leave her alone.

During first period, Mila had sat with her head down. She was trying to control her emotions. It was only Wednesday, and she missed home. Mrs. Marks asked her to pick her head up. Mila didn't move. Mrs. Marks kept asking. Mila got angry and yelled at her. She told Mrs. Marks that her husband had died to get away from her. Mrs. Marks's husband had passed away last month. Mila really didn't mean it, but she didn't have time to explain. With tears in her eyes, the teacher sent her to see the principal.

She stood there for a moment and looked at Mr. Stride. He looked tired, and his suit jacket was too big. The sleeves covered his hands. *This school is stupid*, Mila thought. Mr. Stride opened the door, and Mila walked in.

There were ten other kids in the room. Mila had never been in such a small class before. They all looked over at her. They looked angry and tough. She did not belong in 4B, she thought. The teacher came over to her.

"Hi, Mila. I'm Miss Andrews." Miss Andrews looked young and had short brown hair. Her face was round.

"Hi," Mila mumbled. She looked around the room. The biggest kid in class was throwing paper balls at another student. The smaller kid turned around and stared at him. The big kid threw a ball right between his eyes. Another woman walked over and took the paper from him.

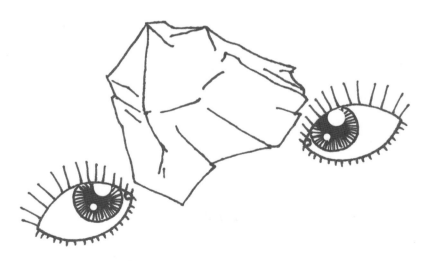

"That's Mrs. Taylor. She's the teacher aide for our room. If I'm busy and you need something, you can ask her."

Miss Andrews pointed to a desk. A dark-haired girl was sitting next to it. Her head was down on her arm. "This one will be yours. You can take a seat." Miss Andrews stood over the girl. "Jayme, sit up. We're going to start our next lesson."

The girl mumbled something. She rubbed her eyes. There was a button imprint on her forehead.

"I'm not staying here," Mila said, making her voice firm. There was no reason to be nice.

Miss Andrews nodded. "I understand you aren't happy. Why don't you try it out for now and see? Maybe you'll end up liking it here."

Clearly Miss Andrews wasn't going to listen to her. Mila sat down. She was sure she wasn't going to like it here. The kids in this room were mean or stupid. Or both. Mila was neither of those things.

She and her friends would laugh about this. That is, if they were here. They would say that Mila should not be in 4B. She was too popular. Too well-liked. She was a cheerleader! These teachers were crazy.

The girl next to her turned.

"Hey," she said. "I'm Jayme."

Mila didn't say anything. She wasn't here to make friends. The girl put her head back down. Times like this made Mila mad at her mom. How could she do this to Mila? She screwed up everything. And now Mila had to pay for her mistakes by having to move to a new town. New town, new house, new school. She wished she could talk to Alicia.

Alicia was her best friend. They had been cheerleading co-captains the year before. She was very funny. Alicia would be able to say something to make her laugh. Instead, she was stuck at this school with no one on her side.

Miss Andrews walked to the front of the room. "Okay, class, let's take out our English books."

Mila heard a few kids sigh. She took her book out from her bag.

"Mila, why don't you start us off? We're on chapter three."

Mila read a few pages of the chapter. Miss Andrews called on a student named Landon to take over. He was pretty bad at reading. He stumbled over a lot of the words. A couple other kids laughed. Mila felt bad.

Mila stared out the window. The tree branches were moving in the wind. A few leaves flew through the air. It was fall. Football season. The most exciting time of the year. Her friends would be getting ready for the game on Friday. It would be the first time she missed one.

There are only two more classes before lunch, she thought. She would need to buy something to eat. Her aunt had packed her a turkey sandwich. She didn't know Mila was a vegetarian.

Just another person who didn't understand her.

Chapter Two:
Leaving Home

They took Mila from her home on a Thursday afternoon. She knew something wasn't right when she got there. A strange car was in the driveway. She opened the door and saw two strangers in the kitchen. A woman sat at the table. A man stood looking out the window. Her mother wasn't there.

At first, they seemed friendly. The woman gave her name. She asked Mila to sit down. Mila sat without taking her coat off. She remembered because it was a big coat and the chair arms squeezed it around her. It made her feel better. She put her book bag on her lap and waited. The woman half-smiled at her.

"Your mom has been having a hard time," the woman said.

Mila had forgotten the woman's name. It was something annoyingly happy like Daisy or Annie. Mila wasn't sure if she should agree with her or not. She nodded a little.

"This morning, she decided to get help. She checked into treatment."

Daisy paused again. Mila's arms were around her book bag. She was confused. Why were they telling her this? What was going on?

"Your mom will be gone for a while. Since we can't find your dad, we called your aunt. She agreed to take you while your mom gets better. We're here to take you there."

This can't be right, Mila thought. Sure, her mom drank a lot. Sometimes she would drink instead of eating dinner. And sometimes it was hard to wake her up in the morning. But they were handling it. Mila was taking care of her. Anyway, her mom wouldn't leave without telling her. And they couldn't expect her to live with her aunt. She barely knew her aunt. Mila felt her face get hot. Her heart pounded against her bag. She hugged it tighter.

"What if I don't want to go?" she asked the woman.

The smile left the woman's face.

"You don't have a choice. You can't stay here," she said. "If you come with us, you'll have time to pack. If not, we'll have to pack for you."

The man turned to stand by the woman. Mila knew she didn't have a choice. He was very tall and very big.

Mila was sure he would make her go.
She nodded and pushed herself up from
the chair.

Daisy followed her. She talked as Mila packed, but Mila didn't listen. She felt empty and alone. Her heart sank into her stomach. She wasn't sure what to take. She had never been away from home for long. There were a few sweaters on her dresser. She stuffed them into her bag.

The ride to her aunt's house was six hours. She sat in the back seat. The woman sat in front of her, and the man drove. Mila's heart fell when they got to the highway. This was real. Strangers were taking her to live with a stranger.

"What about my school?" she asked.

"You'll go to a school near your aunt. We talked to the principal this morning. Everything is ready for you to start on Monday. No need to worry." Daisy's smile had returned since they left. "We'll finish packing your things and send them to you."

It was nighttime when Mila felt the car stop. They were parked outside a house. She looked out the window. It was a small house. The lights were on. She could see someone walk to the front door.

"Time to get out, Mila." Daisy opened the door for her.

Mila got out of the car. They walked up to the house together. The front door opened. Mila's aunt was on the other side.

"Hi, honey," Aunt Julie said.

Aunt Julie didn't look anything like Mila's mom. Mila had been a little kid the last time she saw her aunt. Neither of them looked the same anymore.

"I'm so glad to see you. But sad to hear about your mom." She frowned.

"We have a couple more things to go over," Daisy said. "Do you have a minute?"

"Sure, come on in."

Mila walked into the house. Daisy followed. The house was small but cozy. The living room was to the right. A gray cat lay on the couch. It looked up when they walked in.

"We can sit in the kitchen," Aunt Julie said. "Mila, your room is the first door on the right." She pointed to a hallway.

Mila walked over to the room. There was a quilt on the bed and a large painting on the wall. It showed a house with a path that led into a forest. Mila thought it looked like something you would see at a museum. Very old and boring.

She threw her bag onto a chair in the corner. She lay down on the bed. This all felt like a bad dream. She had just talked to her mom the night before. She had been lying on the couch watching TV. Mila had kissed her goodnight and gone to bed.

When she woke up, her mom wasn't there. Mila guessed she had gone out for more alcohol. She never thought her mother would have left her.

Mila pulled out her phone and dialed her mom's number. It went to voicemail right away. She threw the phone on the floor and pushed her face into the pillow.

Chapter Three:
Two Weeks

Mila threw her lunch bag onto the counter. She heard her aunt in the back room.

"How was your day?" Aunt Julie yelled.

"Terrible," said Mila.

Her aunt came into the kitchen. She wore a large white shirt over jeans. Her hands and clothes were covered in paint.

"I'm sorry to hear that."

Her aunt stood there. She wiped her hands on her shirt. Mila thought she looked unsure of what to say.

"Are you hungry? I can start something for dinner."

"No," said Mila. "And I don't eat meat."

"Wait, what?"

"I'm a vegetarian. You put a turkey sandwich in my lunch."

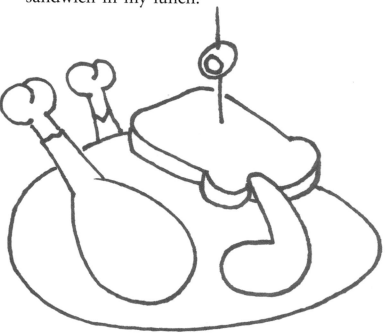

You would know that if you ever came to visit, Mila thought. She turned down the hallway and into her room. She flung her book bag onto the chair. The people from social services had sent her other clothes. They were in boxes on the floor. *I might as well unpack*, she thought. It was annoying to live out of boxes and bags.

One of the boxes had things from her desk. There were pens, books, and pictures. One was a picture she thought was her dad. Her mom had never told her much about him. He had left before Mila was born. All her mom said was that he lived in Nevada. He owned an auto repair shop. He had another family. Mila thought it was weird social services couldn't find him. But she knew living with him wouldn't be any better. He knew her less than Aunt Julie.

There was a knock at her door.

"Hey, kiddo. I'm sorry about lunch," Aunt Julie said. She had changed into clean clothes. "Is it okay if I come in?"

"Fine."

Aunt Julie moved the book bag and sat on the chair.

"I know this is strange. And I don't know you very well. I'm hoping we can change that."

"Have you heard from my mom?" Mila said, putting clothes away in the dresser.

"Not from her, but from the staff. They say she is doing okay."

"And they think she'll be there for a couple weeks?"

"Probably, yes."

"Okay." Mila could deal with this for 14 more days.

Aunt Julie's cat, Beau, came into the room. He jumped onto the bed.

"Beau, what are you doing?" Aunt Julie went to pick him up.

"He can stay," Mila said. She sat down to pet him.

"How's spaghetti for dinner? No meatballs."

"That's fine. I'm going to do my homework."

"Okay, hon." Aunt Julie stood up and then paused. She looked like she wanted to hug Mila. "I'll let you know when it's ready."

Mila opened her planner. She started numbering the days until two weeks. Tomorrow she would go see Mr. Stride. She would make her case about leaving 4B.

"What do you think, Beau? Think they'll let me out of that prison?"

Beau stood up and stretched his back. He laid back down and went to sleep.

The next day, Aunt Julie drove Mila to school. Aunt Julie's hours at the art gallery were always different. On the mornings she worked, she drove Mila. It was quicker than taking the bus.

Mila went right to Mr. Stride's office. "Can I help you?" said the secretary. "I'd like to talk to Mr. Stride."

"Do you have an appointment?"

"No, but I need to talk to him." *Who knew you needed an appointment?* Mila thought. Was he really that busy?

"He's with a student right now. Write your name and homeroom number down. I'll give him the message."

She handed Mila paper and a pen.

The class had started when Mila got to 4B. Miss Andrews was reviewing math problems. Mila gave Miss Andrews her late pass.

"Thanks, Mila. We've just started. We're reviewing for the quiz on Friday."

Mila sat down in her seat. Only a couple of kids were paying attention. Jayme was sleeping again. The big kid Mila saw on her first day was drawing on his desk. His name was Jordan. Mrs. Taylor turned to Jordan and told him to stop. He threw his pen on the floor and walked out the door. Mrs. Taylor followed. *She's like a guard*, thought Mila. *Chasing after kids to bring them back to prison.*

Miss Andrews went back to the board. Mila thought it was stupid how she taught. She spent too much time explaining everything. Did she think they were dumb? This stuff was easy. Mila didn't take any notes. She saw Landon looking at her. He had bright blue eyes. He quickly turned away when she looked back at him.

Someone knocked on the classroom door. Miss Andrews answered it. It was one of the hall monitors, named Miss Nancy.

"Mr. Stride's secretary sent me for Mila. He can meet with her now."

Mila popped up. This was her chance!

"I'll walk you to the office," Miss Nancy said.

I don't need to be walked there, Mila thought. She wasn't a baby. She could walk there on her own. But she guessed they wouldn't trust her to walk by herself anymore. She was a 4B kid now.

Mr. Stride was sitting at his desk when she walked in.

"What can I do for you, Miss Hernandez?"

"I don't belong in 4B. I tried it for a day. But I think I should go back to Mrs. Marks's class."

Mr. Stride slowly closed and opened his eyes. He put his folded hands on the desk.

"I know you don't want to be there, Mila. But that's the best place for you. Miss Andrews is a great teacher. Do you not like her?"

"No, she's okay," said Mila.

"Have any kids been mean to you?"

"No."

"Are you not learning anything?"

Mila thought about the math lesson this morning. It was pretty easy. But it wasn't about the lesson.

"No, it's not that."

"Then what is it?"

Mila didn't know how to say it. She didn't like being treated differently. She didn't like being labeled as a problem kid. She was angry she was even at this school. It made it even worse that she wasn't in a regular classroom. She couldn't even try to blend in. But Mr. Stride was right. There was nothing really wrong with 4B. She just didn't like it.

"I guess it's nothing," said Mila.

"Okay, well, that settles it. Back to your classroom. And have a good day!"

Mila walked back to 4B. *Fourteen days*, she thought. *I can deal with it until then.*

Chapter Four:
Dinner with Patrick

Mila slept in on Saturday. When she woke up, she forgot where she was. The painting of the house on the wall reminded her. Her aunt's name was in the corner. Aunt Julie's house was full of her paintings. She had gone to school for art. She told Mila that she hoped to have a show at a gallery one day. Until then, she just worked in one.

Mila got out of bed. She looked at herself in the mirror. Her dark hair was a mess. She had forgotten to brush it before she went to bed. Mila heard the front door slam shut. Aunt Julie must have been out.

She twisted her hair into a braid and went into the kitchen.

"Good morning, sleepyhead," Aunt Julie said. She was putting groceries away. "Or should I say, good afternoon?"

Mila checked the clock on the oven. It was after noon.

"I didn't know I slept so late." Mila pulled out a stool and sat at the counter.

"Not a problem. I went to the store and got some things. Are these okay?" She held up a pack of veggie burgers.

"Yeah, those are fine," said Mila.

Aunt Julie finished putting everything away. She stuffed the bags under the sink.

"Is it okay if my boyfriend comes for dinner?" Aunt Julie asked. "He comes over on Saturdays. I just want to make sure it's okay with you. I know you're still not used to being here."

"What are you making for dinner?"

"I haven't decided yet. Do you think you can help me? I'm not used to meatless cooking. I don't want to keep making pasta for you."

"Yeah," said Mila. She wasn't surprised to hear her aunt didn't have a clue. She mostly ate things that came from a box.

"Do you have rice? Veggies?"

"Check and check."

"You can make fried rice."

"Sounds like a plan."

Aunt Julie's boyfriend came over around dinnertime. He was tall and thin. He had messy brown hair and glasses. He and Aunt Julie seemed to fit together well. He was tall and awkward and she was tall and graceful. They balanced each other out.

"I'm sorry I'm late. My last patient was very difficult. He kept trying to run away from me." He gave Aunt Julie a quick kiss.

"That's all right. I just finished making dinner. Mila, this is Patrick."

"Nice to meet you, Mila. I've heard a lot about you."

Mila looked at him, confused. "Your patient tried to run away?"

"Oh right. I'm a vet. My last patient was a cat. He did *not* want his claws trimmed."

"That makes more sense," said Mila.

"Speaking of cats, how's this guy?" He picked up Beau. "His eye looks a lot better."

"The eye drops helped a lot," said Aunt Julie, "Thanks for getting them for me. Take a seat. Dinner is ready."

Mila sat at the table. She felt weird. Aunt Julie and Patrick knew each other well. Mila didn't know either of them. And they didn't know her. She felt like she was crashing their dinner. Aunt Julie spooned rice onto her plate. She talked with Patrick about work.

Mila would never admit this. But it felt good to sit down and have dinner together. Mila and her mom used to do that every night. But over the past month,

Mila's mom had stopped eating at the table with her. She had stopped eating much at all. Instead, she drank until she fell asleep on the couch.

"So Mila, what do you do for fun?" Patrick said, taking a bite of food.

"Lots of things. Hang out with friends, go shopping. I'm also a cheerleader."

"A cheerleader? I can't imagine flipping around like that."

"Yeah, it takes a lot of practice."

Mila moved her food around on her plate. *Aunt Julie could have cooked this a little longer*, she thought.

"I can imagine. I think I'm far too tall to do anything like that. Track was much more my sport."

Mila's phone rang. She pulled it out of her pocket. It was Alicia.

"I have to take this," she said.

Mila ran into her bedroom to answer the call. She was so happy to hear from her best friend. Alicia would understand her. She would make her feel better.

"Hey!"

"Hey, girl. How are you? Where have you been?"

"They took me away," Mila said, her throat tight. She sat down on the bed.

"Oh, man. You told me before that your mom was drinking. And then one day you just weren't in school. At first I just thought you were sick or something. Then I saw your house was dark. What happened?"

Mila put a pillow behind her head. She told Alicia everything that had happened. She told her about her mom's treatment. About coming to her aunt's house. Alicia filled her in on what she missed back home. One new girl made the cheerleading team. There were a few new, cute guys at school. One of their classmates got kicked out. They talked for two hours. Mila felt like her old self after talking to Alicia. They made plans to talk again soon.

The next week went a little better. Mila got an 80 on her quiz. She also started talking to a girl in class.

Katie was Mila's age. She sat in front of her. She had a little bit of a lisp. Her "s" sometimes sounded like a "th." But she was funny and easy to talk to. Her family had moved to town recently. They both felt the same way about 4B. It was the worst.

Chapter Five:
Bad News

Friday mornings started with social studies. Miss Andrews was talking about Ellis Island. She talked about how people came to America. Mila wasn't paying attention. She and Katie were talking about the weekend. Katie asked Mila if she wanted to come over after school.

"Mila, you'll want to listen up," said Miss Andrews. "As part of this unit, you will make a poster about your family. You'll each draw your family tree. You'll also write a short family history. Names, jobs, and where everyone came from."

Mila was worried. She didn't know much about her family. How could she write about them? And what would she say about her mom? She couldn't tell the truth. Everyone would judge her. They would think her mom was a bad person. They would think she came from a bad family. *I'll just have to lie about it*, she thought.

"Feel free to work with someone on this project," Miss Andrews said, "They are due a week from today. And let me know if you have any questions."

Katie turned around again. "Well, this is stupid. At least we can work on it together. Do you want to come over?"

Mila didn't want to say yes. She didn't want to tell Katie about her mom. But she also wanted to make a new friend.

"Sure, I'll come. I'll just have to ask my aunt later."

"Girls, please stop talking. I will have to separate you."

Miss Andrews finished up the lesson. Math was next. It was always a stressful subject for everyone. Mrs. Taylor walked around while Miss Andrews taught. Mila wasn't paying attention. She watched as Jordan got angry. He would write something, then cross it out. Finally, he threw his pencil. He put his head down. Mrs. Taylor came over to help.

Mila called her aunt after school. She said it was okay for Mila to go to Katie's. She would pick Mila up later.

"Great, we can walk to my house. It's really close." Katie told her.

Mila packed up her bag. She closed her locker and followed Katie outside.

"It's great to have a friend over. There aren't many *normal* people in 4B. It's so hard to make friends," said Katie.

"How long have you been in 4B?" Mila asked. They stopped at the corner to cross.

"Since we moved here last year. We used to live in California. I miss it. Have you ever been?"

Mila shook her head.

"Oh, it's so amazing! It's always nice out. There's always something fun to do. You should come with us sometime. We're always visiting my grandma."

They crossed the street and turned left. Mila moved her bag on her back. She had never been far from home. Her aunt's house was the farthest she had ever been. She and her mom didn't have a lot of money. They had never gone on vacation. Katie turned into a driveway.

"Here we are. Don't mind the noise. My brother plays the guitar a lot, and my sister is always crying."

They walked through the door. Mila heard the sounds of a guitar. Katie threw her shoes into a corner. The house was big. There was a staircase in the middle. The dining room was to the right. A hallway led to the kitchen on the left. Mila heard a woman yell upstairs. A baby started crying.

"See what I mean?" Katie said, heading upstairs.

They went down the hall to her room. Katie closed the door. She fell onto a chair. Her room had a big bed in the middle. There were two bookshelves. A computer sat on her desk.

"Your house is so awesome," said Mila. She sat on a colorful rug at the end of the bed.

"It's okay. Not as nice as the California house."

Mila started to feel bad. Katie's family was really nice. Her house was really nice. Mila wondered if anyone's family was like hers. Maybe she was the only one in 4B without a dad. Maybe she was the only one whose mom was in treatment. Katie's life seemed perfect. Why would she act out in school?

"Can I ask you a question?" said Mila.

"Sure," Katie said.

"How come you're in 4B?"

"You haven't heard?"

Mila shook her head.

"I punched a girl in Mrs. Marks's class. Then they tried to give me detention. I walked out. So, I got out-of-school suspension. And now I'm stuck in 4B."

"Why did you punch her?"

"She made fun of my accent." Katie always called her lisp an accent. "They say I have anger control issues."

"Now can I ask you a question?" Katie asked. "What do you think of Landon?"

"He's cute, I guess," said Mila.

"I knew it!" said Katie. "I saw him look at you during class."

Aunt Julie came around dinnertime. She looked worried when Mila saw her.

"How was it?" her aunt asked as Mila got in the car.

"Good." Mila threw her bag into the back seat.

"I'm glad," she said. She turned the radio down. "So, I talked to your mom."

Mila felt her face get hot. She thought her mom couldn't talk to anyone. Maybe she just didn't want to talk to *her*.

"She's doing well. She's going very slowly, though. They told her she needs to stay longer."

Mila was afraid to ask. But she did.

"How much longer?"

"She didn't know."

Aunt Julie put her hand over Mila's. Mila pulled hers away. Her heart sank. *This can't be true*. She had thought two weeks at most. Being here longer was too much to think about. Aunt Julie said something. Mila wasn't listening. She looked out the window. She let her eyes get lost in the darkness.

Chapter Six:
Running Away

Mila spent the next day in bed. Beau lay with her. She never wanted to get up again. She would lie here until she could go home. Or she could run away. She had a key to her house. She could catch a bus there. Then she could go to her old school. She would take care of herself until her mom came home. Then she would help take care of her mom again. It was an idea. She would need some money, though. Aunt Julie popped her head in.

"Can I come in?"

Mila didn't say anything. Aunt Julie sat on her bed. Mila turned to face the wall.

"I talked to the doctors today. They said your mom will probably need to stay for another month."

A month? thought Mila. She would have to spend a whole month here? Why was her mom taking so long? Did she not want to come home? She pulled the covers over her head. She felt so powerless. Aunt Julie got up and left the room.

Mila fell asleep. When she woke up, it was dark. Aunt Julie was talking in the kitchen on the landline. Landlines were for old people. Aunt Julie's voice was quiet. Mila heard her name. She got up and stood by the door.

"I know, Mom...I *have* thought of that...No, I haven't said anything to Mila... Because she's only been here a couple of weeks."

There was a phone in Mila's room. She picked it up and turned it on. She heard her grandmother's voice.

"You know how Jackie is. She never asked for help. Always waited until things were bad. Poor Mila. Who knows how long Jackie will be there. Like I said, she might be better with you. I'll look into how to get custody."

Mila dropped the phone. No one was getting custody of her. Her mother was just sick. Once she was better, Mila would leave. They weren't going to take Mila away from her mom. She couldn't trust her aunt.

It would be better if she left. Mila grabbed her shoes and coat. She walked past her aunt.

"I have to go, Mom," she heard her aunt say.

Mila opened the front door and slammed it behind her. She turned down the first road she saw. She didn't want her aunt to find her. She couldn't go to Katie's house. Aunt Julie knew where she lived.

It was late. She didn't know the neighborhood. The streetlights were not very bright. She turned on the light on her phone. There were houses all around her. She was on a street called Mulberry.

Mila was so angry. She didn't care where she went. She just wanted to get away. Far away from this place. From her aunt. From school. Didn't her mom think about her when she left? What did she think would happen to her? She thought they were close. She wasn't sure now. Tears fell down her face. She had walked for about ten minutes. There was a park ahead of her. She sat down on a bench.

The wind blew the tree branches. Her phone rang. It was her aunt. She put the phone on silent. Two months ago, everything was perfect. Her mom had a job. She had just started a new school year. She and Alicia were co-captains. Then her mom was fired and she couldn't find a job. Mila remembered that day.

She got home from school. Her mom was lying on the couch. She was in pajamas. A tissue box was next to her. She stayed like that for a couple of days. Later, her mom applied for lots of other jobs. A couple of places called back. They weren't hiring. Mila had started to worry they would have to sell the house. She wondered if she could get a job. Then her mom started drinking more. Mila found empty bottles hidden in the trash. She knew something was wrong. But she didn't say anything. Maybe this was Mila's fault. Maybe she should have told someone.

Her phone lit up in her hand. A few tears fell on the screen. She wished someone would tell her what to do. She dialed Alicia's number. Alicia could make her feel better. She always did. It rang a few times before she picked up.

"What's going on, Mila?" It was hard to hear. There was loud talking in the background.

"I just found out some bad news. I might have to stay here longer."

"Oh, that really sucks."

Mila heard Alicia say something to someone else.

"Yeah, what's going on with you?"

"I'm at Ray's Pizzeria. We won the game tonight! Look, I have to go. I'll call you again soon." Alicia hung up.

The quiet seemed loud to Mila. She was totally alone. More tears came.

Mila watched a car turn down the street. It pulled up next to her. Aunt Julie got out and opened the passenger door. Mila wiped her eyes and got in.

Chapter Seven:
Trust

They didn't say anything on the way back to the house. It was only a five-minute drive. It felt a lot longer. Mila watched the houses pass. Her aunt pulled into the driveway. She turned the car off. They sat for a minute. It was very quiet.

"I'm not trying to take you from your mom," Aunt Julie said.

Mila looked at her hands. She tried not to cry.

"Your grandmother doesn't always think. She just wants what's best for you. We both do." She moved her keys between her hands. "I'm sorry you heard that."

Mila didn't know what to say. She wanted to believe her aunt. But she was still angry. She didn't know if she could trust her. She didn't know what to think.

"I can understand if you don't trust me anymore," said Aunt Julie.

"It's not just that," said Mila.

She wasn't sure what to say. She felt so many emotions. They felt like a hard ball sitting in her chest. She didn't want to feel this way anymore.

"I'm just so mad," she said, making a fist with her hand. "At everything going on. At everyone. I hate this."

"I'm mad, too. You can even ask Patrick. I was so upset when I got that call," Aunt Julie said. She sighed. "I'm mad your mom didn't call me. I'm mad I didn't know what was going on. I'm mad because she and I aren't close anymore."

Mila didn't know this bothered her aunt. She had never thought about how she felt. Her mom never talked about Aunt Julie. Mila thought they had never gotten along. Maybe there was more to the story.

"I just don't know what to do," said Mila. "It feels like bad things keep happening to me. I don't have any say."

Outside, it started snowing. Big, slow snowflakes fell on the car windows. Mila started to feel cold.

"Why don't you call your mom?" Aunt Julie said. "She told me that you can call now. I think it would be good for both of you. It might make you feel a bit better."

"Yeah, I would like that."

They watched the snow cover the windshield.

"How about we go inside? I'll make us some hot chocolate. And we can eat ice cream and watch TV."

Mila nodded, and they headed inside. She sat down on the couch. Beau came and sat on her lap.

"Cookie dough or cookies and cream?" Aunt Julie asked.

"Cookie dough."

They ate their ice cream in silence. Mila sat on one side of the couch. Aunt Julie was on the other side. She pulled a blanket over them. Beau sat down in the middle. He started purring.

Mila felt a little better after their talk. And she trusted her aunt more. She was glad to hear her mom wanted her to call. But she wasn't sure what to say to her.

She thought about her call with Alicia. Mila was still mad at her. How could Alicia blow her off like that? She was supposed to be her best friend. Now that she needed her, she wasn't there.

They had been friends since second grade. Mila thought they would always be friends. Now she wasn't sure. She thought things would stay the same after she left. Maybe she was wrong. Everything felt so unsure now.

Both Mila and her aunt fell asleep on the couch. The TV was still on. Their empty ice cream bowls lay at their feet.

Chapter Eight:
Mom

Mila was starving when she woke up. She put some bread into the toaster. Aunt Julie was at the table reading a book.

"My neck is killing me," her aunt said. She moved her head from side to side. Her long hair flowed with it. "I think it's mad at me for sleeping on the couch."

Mila laughed. "My back hurt a little when I got up. It's better now."

Mila grabbed her toast and sat at the table.

"Patrick didn't come over yesterday."

"Yeah, I thought maybe it wasn't a good idea," Aunt Julie said.

"Thanks," said Mila. "But I like him."

"I do too," Aunt Julie said, smiling. "I can ask him to come over sometime this week."

"Sure. And I can help you with dinner."

Aunt Julie closed her book.

"How are you feeling today?"

"Better."

"I'm glad." She handed Mila a piece of paper. "This is the number to reach your mom. It connects to the main desk. You have to give them her room number to be connected. It's 323."

Mila took the paper. She had wanted to call her mom for so long. It felt strange to have her number at last. She went to her room. She shut the door behind her.

"Good morning! How can I help you?" The woman on the phone sounded very happy. It wasn't what Mila had expected to hear.

"Room 323, please."

The phone started ringing again. Mila counted. One…two…three…

"Hello?" The voice was very quiet.

"Hi, Mom. It's Mila."

"Mila?" It sounded like she had just woken up. It didn't sound like her mom. "Where are you?"

"I'm at Aunt Julie's house." Her mom should already know that. Maybe she wasn't doing as well as Mila first thought.

"Oh, that's right," she sighed. "I'm sorry. I don't feel well."

"Are you okay, Mom?"

"Yeah, I just need to lie down. How are you?"

"I'm okay." Mila wasn't sure what to say to her.

This didn't sound like her mom. Mila wanted to ask her why she left. But she didn't want to upset her.

"Aunt Julie said you have to stay there longer. She said it might be a month."

"That's what they told me. They don't know for sure."

"When will you know?"

"It depends on how everything goes."

Mila sat on her bed. She had been pacing back and forth.

"What happened? I knew you were sick. But I thought I was taking care of you."

She heard her mom sigh. She was quiet for a minute.

"It was too much, Mila. Too much for me. Too much for you."

"But we've always done everything together." Mila felt tears start to come. She couldn't control her emotions any longer. "Why did you leave me?"

Her mom took a long time to reply. Mila thought she had hung up.

"That morning was the first time I was sober in a while. I looked around the house. There were bottles all over. Probably from the night before. I went to find you. You were sleeping in your bed. Seeing you there made me feel bad. I felt bad about what I was doing to you. I missed how our family was before this.

I left because of you, Mila. Because I want to get better for you. I want us to be a family again. But I need to get better first. And I need help to do that." Her voice faded. She sounded very far away.

"What am I supposed to do?" Mila asked. She felt very small. Like a little kid again.

"There's nothing you need to do. Just be a kid. Hang out with your friends. Worry about school."

"It's not that easy," Mila said. *I miss home*, she wanted to say. She heard someone talking in the background.

"I have to go for now," her mom said, "We'll talk soon."

Mila didn't feel much better after their talk. Her mom seemed so strange. But she was hopeful she would get better soon. Mila wanted things to go back to how they were before.

"There's mail for you," Aunt Julie called out.

Mila went into the kitchen. Aunt Julie handed her a white envelope. The school's logo was in the corner. At first, she was worried. She didn't know what it might be. Mila opened it and found her mid-quarter grades. She hadn't been there long. But she had a B in every subject.

"Not bad," said her aunt, looking over her shoulder.

Mila had never gotten such high grades before.

Chapter Nine:
The Presentation

Mila had almost forgotten about her poster presentation. She saw it written on her planner the day before. So much had been going on. She hadn't even started working on it. Aunt Julie helped her. She took her to the store to get supplies.

Mila drew her tree out on the paper. She put the names of her mom's parents at the top. She didn't know her dad's parents. She listed her parents under that. She put Aunt Julie next to her mom. Beau was listed in small letters under her. Then she put herself at the bottom. Aunt Julie helped her write up a short paragraph. Mila decided not to mention everything about her mom. The class didn't need to know details.

The next day was class presentations. Mila was very nervous about it. She was nervous to talk about her family. She could feel her stomach turn. *I think I might puke*, she thought. It was very unlike her. She usually liked to talk in front of people. Just not about these things.

"Are you okay?" Katie whispered to her.

Mila nodded. She felt sick. Did she have time to run to the bathroom?

"Okay class, we're going to start," said Miss Andrews. "I'm very excited to see your posters. Jayme, why don't you go first?"

Jayme went to the front of the room. Mrs. Taylor held her poster up so they could all see. Jayme's presentation was okay. She talked about her parents. They had divorced earlier that year. Her siblings were younger than her. They all lived with her mom. She babysat them a lot.

Katie went next. She talked about her perfect family. And her California house. And how much better her old school was. Mila saw a few of her classmates roll their eyes. Her accent got worse as she presented. Jordan said something under his breath.

Perfect, CA

"What did you say?" said Katie.

Katie stood in front of Jordan's desk. Mila saw her tense up.

"Nothing."

"Nothing? It didn't sound like nothing."

"Okay, Katie. Why don't you take a seat?" Miss Andrews said, trying to prevent a fight.

"No, tell me," Katie demanded.

"Well, you seem to have so much money," Jordan said, "I'm surprised your parents didn't pay to get your mouth fixed."

Katie jumped at Jordan. Mrs. Taylor grabbed her. Katie fought her as she pulled her from the room.

"All right, class, let's keep going with the presentations," said Miss Andrews. "Jordan, you're next."

Jordan stood up front. Mila had watched him pick on kids before this. It was easy for him. He was taller and bigger than everyone else. Mila thought he might have failed a grade. She remembered that he lived with his mom. It made her feel better she wasn't the only one. His presentation was very short. He didn't talk too much.

Landon went after up him. His blonde hair was perfectly messy. It covered half his forehead. He was a lot shorter than Jordan. But he was still taller than Mila. He looked at Mila. She felt her face get hot. His presentation didn't go very well. He had a hard time talking in front of the class. He paused a lot. Mila didn't care. She still liked him.

Mila went next.

She picked up her poster and walked to the front. Everyone was watching her. Mila looked at the paragraph she had written. She started to talk. The presentation went by very fast. She didn't remember most of it. But she did say her mom was sick. She lived with her aunt. She would move home after her mom got better. She finished her presentation and sat down.

After the presentations were done, Miss Andrews walked them to lunch. Mila sat with Jayme. Katie was still gone. Aunt Julie had packed her a peanut-butter-and-jelly sandwich.

"What did you do this weekend?" asked Jayme.

"Nothing really. Just hung out with my aunt."

Mila decided she wasn't going to tell her what happened. It would be too hard to explain it all.

"It looks like I'll be here longer," Mila said.

"That's exciting," Jayme said. Her mouth was full of sandwich. "Well, actually I'm sure you want to get home. But it's exciting to me and Katie."

Mila laughed.

"Did you see Landon during his presentation? He was totally looking at you the whole time."

"Was not!"

Maybe Landon did like her. *I guess I have something to look forward to here,* thought Mila.

Chapter Ten:
New Beginnings

Patrick came over on Wednesday night. Aunt Julie and Mila had cooked veggie lasagna. It was Mila's mother's recipe. It was also her favorite dish. Mila was setting the table when Patrick arrived.

"It's snowing pretty good out there." He stomped his boots on the rug. His coat was covered in snow.

"Be careful! Don't make a mess."

Aunt Julie went over to take his wet things.

"It smells great in here!"

He sat down at the table. Mila put the lasagna down. It was still hot from the oven. She put out three glasses. Aunt Julie put the water pitcher on the table.

"Well, this is fancy. What's all this for?"

"Mila wanted to treat us. It's a special recipe," said Aunt Julie, taking a seat. She cut the lasagna and put a square on each plate. "We also have dessert."

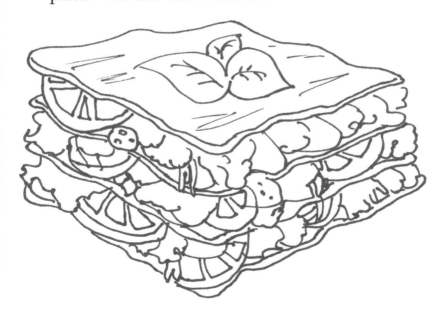

"I'll try to leave room," Patrick said, laughing.

They all dug into the meal. Mila took a bite and let it sit on her tongue. It didn't taste exactly the same as when her mom made it, but it was good. It reminded her of home.

"No angry patients today?" said Mila.

"No, luckily everyone was good. We did have one interesting case though." Patrick said. He finished chewing his bite of food. "Someone brought in their five-year-old golden retriever. His name was Sam. The owners said he had been acting tired and wasn't eating. We did an X-ray on his belly. It showed a pretty big mass, so we took him into surgery. Guess what we found?"

"A hat," Aunt Julie said.

"Socks?" Mila suggested.

"Both good guesses, but no. It was a kitchen towel!"

"Gross," said Mila. "I bet you get to play that game a lot."

"Oh yeah," Patrick said. "It's crazy the things an animal will eat. Speaking of which, this is really good, Mila."

"Thanks. I've never made it before. I'm glad it turned out okay."

Mila remembered hating veggies as a kid. Her mom made the lasagna to get her to eat them. It was funny to think about that now as a vegetarian.

"Your aunt tells me you're really good with Beau. Would you like to come by the office sometime? You could help out around the place. You can even help me take care of the animals."

"Yeah, that would be fun, thanks," Mila said.

The idea of being a vet interested her. It was never something she had thought about before. But after listening to Patrick, it was something she started to think about. She did really like animals. And it seemed like a cool job. There was always something new to do.

Aunt Julie and Patrick chatted a bit more. They talked about some friends and made plans for the weekend. Mila sat and listened. It felt nice to have dinner with them. To have dinner with two other people. She thought about how lucky she was. Yes, her mom was sick. And she had to move to a new town. And a new school. And she still missed her old friends. But she was starting to enjoy this new life. It was not something she'd expected. It was not something she'd wanted. But she liked it all the same. She felt bad for being so cold to Aunt Julie when she first got there.

She was glad she'd gotten to know her better.

Mila heard a knock at the front door. Aunt Julie got up to answer it.

"It's for you, Mila."

It was Katie.

"Hey, my mom was in the area picking up my sister. I remembered that you live near her friend. Do you want to come over for a little bit? We could do our homework together."

Mila turned to her aunt. "Can I go?"

"What about dessert?"

"Save me some?"

"Okay, just call when you want me to come get you. Not too late, though!"

Mila grabbed her coat and headed out the door. She finally felt like she belonged.

Want to Keep Reading?

Turn the page for a sneak peek at
the next book in the series.

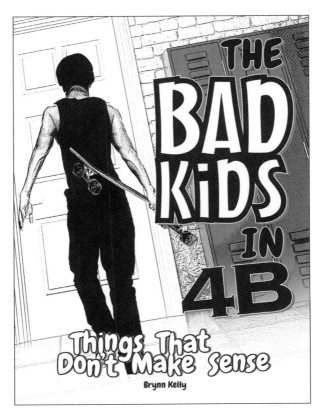

9781538382233

Chapter One:
The Report Card

"Watch out!" said Landon. He jumped onto his bed. "The dragon turned the floor into lava."

Landon's little brother, Jake, jumped after him. Jake loved this game. He was six years old. He spent most of his time playing make-believe. Landon was really good at coming up with the stories. This afternoon, they were knights. They were fighting a dragon. They needed to save their town.

"I'll throw this rock at him," said Jake. He pretended to pick up a rock.

"You'll need something bigger than that."

Jake opened his arms wide. He pretended to pick up a larger rock. Landon laughed.

"Here!" Landon held his hand out. "Take this sword. On the count of three, we'll charge at him."

They stood on the bed ready to attack. Jake held up his arm.

"One, two, three!"

They jumped off the bed and ran toward a chair in the corner. Landon slashed at it. Jake stabbed it with his pretend sword.

"He's dead," said Landon. "Good job, Sir Jake!"

"Time for dinner, boys!" their mom called from downstairs.

"Race?" said Landon.

They ran down the stairs into the kitchen. Landon beat Jake, who came running after. Landon sat down and grabbed his water glass. He was out of breath, but happy.

"I hate when you do that. I've told you that before, Landon. Stop acting like a little kid. You're being a bad influence on your brother. I don't need two crazy boys running around."

His mother put a plate of chicken on the table. Her blonde hair was twisted into a bun. She was wearing a skirt and a buttoned shirt. She looked like she was going out.

"I have to leave in a couple minutes. I have a parent-teacher conference at Jake's school tonight."

It's parent-teacher conference time? Landon thought. Didn't they just have conferences not too long ago? Maybe this was a special one just for Jake. Hopefully Landon's school wasn't having them. Landon had gotten in trouble last time. His parents took away his computer. He wasn't allowed to hang out with his friends for two weeks.

ABOUT THE AUTHOR

Brynn Kelly is a writer from Buffalo, New York, where she studied English and creative writing and received a master's degree in social work. She is the author of three educational books, *The People and Culture of Venezuela*, *The Layers of Earth's Atmosphere*, and *Air Pressure and Wind*. In her free time, she enjoys doing yoga and spending time with her dog, Neno.

Welcome to 4B

Bryna Kelly

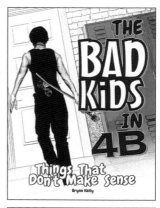

Things That
Don't Make Sense

Bryna Kelly

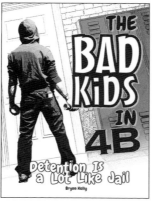

Detention Is
a Lot Like Jail

Bryna Kelly

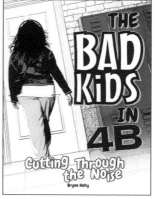

Cutting Through
the Noise

Bryna Kelly

Check out more books at:
www.west44books.com

An imprint of Enslow Publishing

WEST **44** BOOKS™